Warm dog

Biff's huge, slobbery jaw was just a ~~~~ behind us! He was gaining.

So even though I really, *really* didn't want to, I reached down and scooped Princess up. I held her in my arms and barreled at maximum warp.

"GACK! Huh-huh-huh yip! Yip! GACK!"

Princess huffed up her doggie biscuits. She heaved up a hot load of Gravy Train gumbo. She puked her Purina. Right into my neck.

"GACK! Sploot."

Warm dog vomit slid down my neck. It slid down beneath my shirt.

At the same time Princess decided she was just so darned excited, she'd better squirt.

"Ohhhh, *Princess!*" I groaned.

Don't miss any of the books in

—the totally
GROSS
and hilariously funny
new series from Bantam Books!

The Great Puke-off

The Legend of Bigfart

Mucus Mansion

Garbage Time

Dog Doo Afternoon

Coming soon:

To Wee or Not to Wee

Visit Barf-O-Rama—the funniest gross site on the Internet—at:
http://www.bdd.com/barforama

DOG DOO AFTERNOON

BY
PAT POLLARI

BANTAM BOOKS
NEW YORK · TORONTO · LONDON · SYDNEY · AUCKLAND

BARF-O-RAMA: DOG DOO AFTERNOON
A BANTAM BOOK : 0 553 50561 0

First published in USA by Bantam Books, 1996
First publication in Great Britain

PRINTING HISTORY
Bantam edition published 1997

Produced by Daniel Weiss Associates, Inc.
33 West 17th Street, New York, NY 10011, USA.

Bantam Books are published by Transworld Publishers Ltd,
61–63 Uxbridge Road, Ealing, London W5 5SA,
in Australia by Transworld Publishers (Australia) Pty Ltd,
15–25 Helles Avenue, Moorebank, NSW 2170,
and in New Zealand by Transworld Publishers (NZ) Ltd,
3 William Pickering Drive, Albany, Auckland.

Printed and bound in Great Britain by
Cox & Wyman Ltd, Reading, Berkshire.

To Michael

ONE

"Hold on, Princess."

"Yip! Yip! Yip!"

"I said, HOLD ON, you stupid dog! I have to collect your deposit."

I reached into my jacket pocket for a Baggie. It wasn't easy because Princess was yanking on her leash and making that noise she makes.

"Yip! Yip! Yip!"

But finally I got a Baggie out and slipped my free hand inside. With the Baggie over my hand, I bent down to pick up Princess's deposit.

"Deposit." That's what Mrs. Vernaglia calls it. I call it a Lassie loaf. Brown substance à la dog. Chihuahua chocolate.

Mrs. Vernaglia owns Princess. I just *walk*

1

Princess. That's my job. I'm a dog walker. A professional dog walker.

My name is Albert Londer. I'm a fairly normal, average kid. The only difference between me and most kids is that I'm kind of ambitious, you know? I mean, I want to be a millionaire by the time I'm twenty-one. I'll be at least a thousandaire by the time I leave junior high. I figure I can make the rest with plenty of time to spare.

So anyway, it was after school and we were walking through Central Park. Just me and Princess. And I was preparing to collect Princess's dogwurst. Her deposit.

Mrs. Vernaglia insists on seeing each of Princess's deposits. I guess it makes her feel like she's involved. Like she's being a good dog mother by always checking to make sure Princess did her thing.

"Yip! Yip! Yip!"

I was just closing my plastic-coated fingers over the steaming hot Benji bar when I saw him standing there, looking at me.

Myron Schwartz.

When he's by himself, Myron is the biggest

wimp in the world. Unfortunately, Myron was not alone. Biff was with him.

Biff is a dog. But not a dog like Princess.

See, Biff thinks Princess is lunch. That's because Biff is to Princess what a jumbo jet is to a paper airplane. Biff is to Princess what an aircraft carrier is to the rubber ducky you play with in the tub.

Biff is large. Biff could give kids pony rides. If you strapped a long nose on Biff, he could pass for an elephant. Biff is so big that once when a car hit him, the car was destroyed and Biff just walked away.

Big. Very big. And with big teeth.

So there I was, bent over, with my Baggie-covered fingers closing around a moist dog-wurst while Princess yip-yip-yipped like a lunatic and yanked on her leash.

"It's Albert and his wimpy dog!" Myron crowed.

"Don't bring that monster near Princess!" I warned him. "Or . . ." But I couldn't really think of a good *or*.

"Or what?" Myron asked. "You'll sic that little rat on me?"

"Myron, you better back off!"

Myron grinned. He let go of Biff's leash. "Get 'em, boy!"

Biff licked his big, sloppy jowls.

He fixed his red-rimmed eyes on me.

He bounded forward!

"Yaaahhh!" I yelled. I took off. I hauled. I relocated at top speed. I worked my Nikes. I did a Road Runner.

But Princess just dragged behind me, bouncing roughly over the ground, yip-yip-yipping at the top of her tiny little lungs.

This would never do. Mrs. Vernaglia was sure to notice if I showed up with Princess dead from being dragged across the rocks and dirt and shrubs and beer cans of the park.

That was like the first rule of professional dog walking: don't kill the dog.

But Biff was hot on my tail.

"Go, boy!" Myron yelled. "Chew 'em up!"

"Yip! Yip! Yip!"

Biff, by the way, does not go, Yip! Yip! Yip!

Biff says, "RAWWRRAWW GRAAWWRR ROWROWROW RRRAWWR!"

4

At the same time I was yelling, "Yaaahhh! No! No! No!"

Biff's huge, slobbery jaw was just a few feet behind us! He was gaining. I wouldn't make it to the door of Mrs. Vernaglia's building in time. Especially since I had to cross a busy street. And I knew that dragging a limp Chihuahua through traffic was probably not a great idea.

So even though I really, *really* didn't want to, I reached down and scooped Princess up. I held her in my arms and barreled at maximum warp.

There was a reason why I didn't want to lift Princess up. Princess has a little problem. She is very excitable. And when she gets excited, she fires whatever she has to fire. It's like she has to get rid of any regrettable fluids she may have handy.

"*GACK! Huh-huh-huh yip! Yip! GACK!*"

Princess huffed up her doggie biscuits. She heaved up a hot load of Gravy Train gumbo. She puked her Purina. Right into my neck.

"*GACK! Sploot.*"

Warm dog vomit slid down my neck. It slid down beneath my shirt.

At the same time Princess decided she was just so darned excited, she'd better squirt.

"Ohhhh, *Princess!*" I groaned.

So there I was. Racing through the streets of the city with a yip! yip! yipping, squirting, magooing rat dog in one hand, a fistful of warm pooptonium in the other hand, and a huge Monster Dog from the Fiery Pits trying to chew my hinder.

But at least I was making money. And that's the important thing.

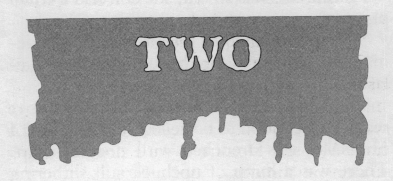
TWO

"Princess!" Mrs. Vernaglia shrieked. "You're upset! Someone has upset my baby!"

"Yip! Yip! Yip!"

I had reached Mrs. Vernaglia's apartment. The maid let me in and I went straight to Mrs. Vernaglia's bedroom. That's where she always was: the bedroom.

She was propped up on about twenty silk pillows. She was wearing a fancy robe and watching the home shopping channel on her TV.

She was old. Very old.

How old? So old that when she was a kid, she had a pet dinosaur. So old that Lewis and Clark were lost exploring her wrinkles.

I mean, she was so old, she still had a *record* player.

"What happened to my Princess?" she demanded, glaring at me through her false eyelashes.

"She's fine, Mrs. Vernaglia," I lied. I wasn't really in the mood to be yelled at. The front of my jacket was drenched with doggie squirt. There was a lump of upchuck still slithering down my chest and starting to get cold. And I was getting a draft from the hole Biff had chewed in my jeans. The back of my jeans looked like I'd blown a jet fart and ruptured the material.

"She's NOT fine! I can tell when my baby has been upset by something. A mother *knows* these things. Just listen to her voice."

"Yip! Yip! Yip!"

"Yes, ma'am," I said, because I couldn't think of anything better to say.

But Mrs. Vernaglia was just getting more and more upset. I dreaded this because I'd seen Mrs. Vernaglia upset before. When she got upset, things started to happen. Gross things. One gross thing in particular.

"She is in distress! She is frantic! I believe she has been badly abused!"

"Not as badly as she deserves to be abused, the obnoxious little rat dog," I said. "What she deserves is for Biff to catch her, chew her into dog burger, and then grill her on the barbecue."

Okay, I didn't *actually* say that. I wanted to say that, but Mrs. Vernaglia pays me really well. And it's just dumb ever to argue with someone who gives you money.

So what I really said was, "Mrs. Vernaglia, you know I am always very, very careful with Princess."

"I don't—" And then it happened. The thing I'd been afraid of. The thing that always seems to happen when Mrs. Vernaglia starts yelling.

She was starting to say, "I don't think you know how precious my little Princess is," but suddenly she was saying, "I don't th-clink you clap-know how prec-clack-clack-ious my clickle Princ-cless is!"

See, Mrs. Vernaglia's upper teeth had fallen out. The glue that held her dentures in

9

popped loose. And now, as she ranted and raved, she was literally chewing her own clacking teeth.

As she yelled her bottom teeth came loose too. Soon she was clacking and clicking while drool formed into foam and dribbled down her wrinkled chin.

It was not a pretty sight.

It's not something you want to see—pink gums and big yellowed teeth clapping loose behind bright red lipstick as flecks of angry spit go flying around like crazed missiles.

But eventually she calmed down.

"Cleck me sklee herck dep-closkit," Mrs. Vernaglia said, and she held out her hand toward me.

"What?" I asked.

Mrs. Vernaglia rolled her eyes. She leaned over and spit her teeth out into her hand. They lay there, glistening in her palm.

"Here-wuh, take fheefh."

Which was toothless-speak for, "Here, take these."

By which she meant her teeth.

She handed me the gooey gums and I took

10

them. I wasn't happy about it, but I took them. I tried not to look down, but I just couldn't help myself.

There was chocolate stuck in the cracks of the molars.

Oh. Oh, gross. Beyond gross. I could feel my stomach squishing, getting ready.

I felt the beginnings of the gack dance—the spazzing of the throat, the waffling of the stomach, the crazed back and forth of the tongue.

The urge to purge was powerful. I could feel her teeth in my hand! I could *feel* them!

But I knew if I did the blew magoo, it would be all over. Mrs. Vernaglia was sure to be insulted if I blew chunks all over the place.

I fought it down! I resisted. I tried to stop the music of the gack dance.

"*Gumph-bleah.*" A small, force-three barficane. The barest surge into the back of my mouth. Just a "taster," as the experts call it.

"What?" Mrs. Vernaglia asked.

"Nothing." I shook my head and swallowed a couple more times.

"Now, let me hee Prinhefhefh depofhit."

In case you don't speak toothless, I will translate. What she said was, "Now, let me see Princess's deposit."

I held out the little plastic bag of dog sausage. She leaned forward and poked at it with her incredibly long, bright, wickedly curved finger-nails.

The doggie sausage mushed and squished as she poked it through the plastic.

"Well, her deposit seems healthy," Mrs. Vernaglia said.

"Yes ma'am," I quickly agreed. "Her deposit was absolutely excellent." I smiled.

"Still, she seems agitated to me." (I'm still translating from toothless.)

I said, "How can you tell? For crying out loud, all the little rat dog ever does is yip-yip-yip and poop-poop-poop and magoo all down the front of me! She's the most disgusting animal alive!"

Okay, okay, I didn't *exactly* say that. I wanted to, but I didn't. Because it was payday.

What I really said was, "Well, you're her mother. I guess you would know if she was upset."

This made Mrs. Vernaglia happy.

Which was too bad, because she smiled at me.

Without teeth.

"I think this would be a good time to give Princess a special present I've been saving up for her. Get it for me. It's the wrapped package over on the dresser."

"Would you like me to put your . . . your teeth . . . over there too?" I asked hopefully.

"No, just hang on to those."

So I got the package. And I held on to the teeth.

Mrs. Vernaglia unwrapped the package. It was small, rectangular, kind of long.

She lifted off the lid.

What was inside was so bright, it almost blinded me. Diamonds! Hundreds of diamonds! A big, thick, glittering necklace of diamonds!

Only it wasn't exactly a necklace.

"Come to me, my little Princess," Mrs. Vernaglia cooed. She lifted the diamonds out of the box and wrapped them around the Chihuahua's pencil-thin neck.

"It's Princess's new collar. Isn't it beautiful?" Mrs. Vernaglia demanded.

"Yes. It's very beautiful." I meant it. It was.

"It ought to be. It cost a hundred thousand dollars."

"A hundred . . . thousand . . ."

"You'll have to be extra careful when you walk Princess now," Mrs. Vernaglia said. "You can't let her lose the collar. Unless you want to have to replace it."

"Um, Mrs. Vernaglia, maybe we could just—" I was going to say, Maybe when she went out, Princess could leave the collar at home. Somewhere safe.

"My little baby wears diamonds just like the royalty she is." She goo-gooed for the dog, holding its jerky little head between her big gnarled hands.

No way, I thought. This is nuts. No way am I walking a dog with a hundred-thousand-dollar collar. Not with Myron and Biff, the Dog from Hades, around.

I had to quit. Didn't I?

"Albert? I meant to tell you. I'll be going into the hospital for a day, this Saturday. A little cosmetic surgery, nothing serious."

She waited like she expected me to say, "Oh no, you don't need cosmetic surgery." But I was too busy thinking, "Mrs. Vernaglia, you don't need a surgeon for your face—you need a mask." In the end I just smiled.

"On Saturday you will have to let yourself in to take Princess for her walk. And then you must care for her all day. I will trust you with the key."

I was still thinking about that stupid collar. No way could I take the risk. If I lost that collar, I'd be paying Mrs. Vernaglia back forever. I had to refuse. I had to stand up for myself.

"Naturally, since this is extra responsibility for you, I am going to pay you a bonus."

My ears pricked up. Bonus?

"One hundred dollars for taking such good care of my baby."

Suddenly I changed my mind. I didn't have to stand up for myself after all.

Not when I was going to make a hundred bucks.

THREE

My mom tells me I should feel sorry for Myron. She says he's just insecure. She says he's just jealous of me.

Yeah, right.

Myron is evil made flesh. Period. Just because he's a little guy doesn't mean he can't be rotten. Just because he's the kind of kid who makes adults go, "Oh, he's so cute," does not mean he isn't a truly creepy person.

I knew I wanted revenge. I just didn't know how to get it.

Until the next morning in class.

"Class? Today, as part of our section on biology, we will be dissecting a frog," said my teacher, Mr. Voigt.

Hello! I thought. I believe I hear opportunity knocking.

"Now, I know some of you will think it's gross to cut open a frog, to stick pins in its heart and liver and other internal organs . . ."

"Mmmmpphh!" That was Dawn Garcia, the girl who sits next to me. She covered her mouth with her hand and looked like she was about ready to launch her lunch into low orbit.

Other kids said, "Ewww."

So I guess Mr. Voigt was right. Some people *would* think it was gross.

"The frogs have been pickled in formaldehyde. We don't have quite enough frogs for everyone, so you will have to share."

Dawn looked at me pleadingly. She has brown hair and kind of green eyes.

Oh, wait. I just remembered. She has *blue* eyes. I guess they just *looked* green because she was imagining slicing and dicing a frog.

"Will you do it?" she asked me.

I shrugged. "Sure. Why not?"

She looked grateful. I wondered if I could

get her to pay me for doing it. Maybe a dollar or two.

Mr. Voigt handed out these little trays with wax on the bottom and pins and a cool scalpel. I used it to carve my name in the edge of my desk. It was kind of hard, though, so I stopped after "Al." I never go by "Al," but the "bert" part would have taken forever.

Then, at last, came the frogs.

They were in a big, huge glass jar. Like twenty of them, all green and dead looking, floating around in the formaldehyde.

Dawn moaned. "Ooooohhh."

That's when it came to me. My plan. I would have my revenge on Myron.

"Look," I whispered to Dawn. "I'll do this for you, and you won't even have to watch. But then I have something I need you to do for me."

She looked at me with nauseous yet suspicious eyes. "Like what?"

"It's not going to be any kind of big deal. I promise. Just a little favor."

"Okay," Dawn said.

The jar of frogs came near and I had to

18

reach in with a pair of long tweezers and select my victim. I grabbed one that looked pretty laid back. I mean, okay, he was dead, so of course he looked casual. But some of the frogs still had these startled expressions. You know, like they were thinking, "Whoa! How did I end up here?"

I squeezed one leg between the tweezers and lifted him out of the jar.

I plopped him in the tray, belly-up.

"Oooohhhhh!" Dawn moaned again.

"Don't look if it's going to make you sick," I said. I was starting to worry that she might actually hurl.

"I just keep thinking: what if he was a person?"

"He wouldn't fit in the tray, that's for sure," I joked. Unfortunately Dawn didn't see the humor. "Let's give him a name," I suggested. I grinned. "I know. Myron. We'll call this frog Myron."

Dawn raised an eyebrow. "Why? Don't you *like* Myron?"

"No. In fact, I can't stand him. I dislike him extremely."

19

"Me too."

I looked at her in total shock. "Huh? You don't like Myron either?"

"I despise Myron," she said with a sudden flash of total despisal. "Do you know what he did to me?"

"No. Tell me, and I'll slice Myron the Frog open."

"It was a few years ago, when I invited him over to a birthday party at my house. My mom gave me this doll. It was a beautiful doll. I mean, I was just a kid, okay? But this was a great doll. I only had her for a few minutes, but already she was like part of my family. I named her Frieda. Frieda Garcia."

There was a dangerous, slightly insane look in Dawn's eyes. "Frieda," she repeated. "I loved that doll. But Myron decided it would be funny to give my doll to his dog."

"Biff," I sneered.

Dawn gaped at me. "Biff? You know about Biff?"

"Oh, yeah. I know all about Biff," I said. "Little Myron and Big Biff."

"That dog ate my doll. I don't mean that

he just bit her or tore her dress. He *ate* her. Ate all of her. Except for her head, which fell off."

"You should have made him pay you back."

"There are some things that money can't buy," Dawn said.

Then I *knew* she was slightly nuts. I mean, money can buy anything.

Dawn hesitated. Then she bent down and opened her backpack. She reached inside. She pulled out her hand, with the fist clenched.

She turned her hand over and opened her fist. Then I saw it. The head.

The head of Frieda Garcia.

There was a dangerous light shining in Dawn's blue, occasionally green eyes. "I carry it with me everywhere. A reminder."

She stared across the room at the back of Myron's head.

"Dawn? You know how I said if I took care of dissecting the frog, I needed you to do something for me?"

"Yes?"

"It involved getting major revenge on Myron. Sound good?"

"I'm in," she said. "What's your plan?"

I told her.

She grinned and laughed a kind of sinister laugh. You know, like one of those bad guys in a cable movie? Like, "Nyahh ha ha ha HA!"

Slightly frightening. But cool.

FOUR

Soon I had the frog laid out nicely with pins stuck into various body parts. All frog guts look pretty much the same to me, so I mostly just stuck the pins in any old place. I mean, come on. How can you tell a frog liver from a frog stomach?

Well, okay, it turns out Mr. Voigt could tell the difference. So he only gave Dawn and me a C-plus. But neither of us really cared. We had other things on our minds.

"Okay, class, come to the front and dump your frogs into this trash can," Mr. Voigt said.

"Now!" I hissed to Dawn.

Everyone was crowding up to the front of the room around the trash can, dumping mangled frogs in. Myron was right in the middle of the crowd.

Dawn ran quickly to stand behind him.

I raced across the room, trying not to look too suspicious. I glanced up to the front. Myron was still trying to reach the trash.

Just beside Myron's desk was his backpack. I knew what was in it.

Lunch.

I reached in and yanked out Myron's lunch bag. Swiftly I opened it and found a sandwich. Ham and cheese. Plenty of mustard. That was good. Mustard would help disguise the flavor.

I slipped the ham out of the sandwich.

I picked up my mangled frog.

I glanced again toward the front of the classroom. Myron had dumped his frog! He was turning, as if to come back.

But there was Dawn! She was talking to him. I could just barely hear what she was saying. Something about how much she liked him.

Yeah, right, I thought grimly.

I lifted the frog from the tray. I had taken

all the pins out, of course. I'm not cruel, after all.

Smooth as a cat burglar I slipped the frog between the two pieces of bread.

Then I hesitated. Should I leave the cheese?

Frog sandwich? Or frog and cheese? Which was grosser?

I checked out the cheese. It was Velveeta. Okay, definitely grosser *with* the cheese.

I put the sandwich back together. I slipped it back in the sandwich bag. Then I shoved the sandwich bag back in the lunch bag and the lunch bag back in the backpack.

Just in time!

"Hey, what are you doing hanging around my desk?" Myron demanded.

Dawn was just beside him, still trying to distract him.

"Oh, is this your desk?" I asked Myron, trying to sound innocent.

He glared at me. His eyes flicked to his bag. He suspected something! He was going to check his bag. My revenge would be ruined!

"Myron?" Dawn said quickly. "How's Biff doing?"

Myron hesitated. "Fine." Then a slow, cruel grin spread across his devil-child face. "In fact, you should have seen him yesterday. He chewed a hole in Albert's pants. Ha ha! You should have seen it!"

Dawn pretended to laugh along. "I'll bet it was funny."

I sent her a wink. That was quick thinking, distracting him that way.

I was getting so I kind of liked this girl.

Myron got so involved in giggling and snorting out his story about me and Princess running from Biff that he totally forgot his suspicions.

Which was unfortunate for him.

An hour later we were in the lunchroom. Dawn and I sat together. We carefully picked a seat where we could see Myron but not be too close to him.

We figured being close might be a bad idea.

The school meal was beef Stroganoff. It was the kind of meal that made me jealous of the kids who brown-bag their lunches.

I ate some of the Stroganoff, but mostly I just waited.

26

"He's opening his lunch bag," Dawn hissed.

"This is where it could all go wrong," I whispered.

"He's opening the sandwich bag!" Dawn said. She grabbed my hand and squeezed. This kind of surprised me, so I almost missed the big moment.

"This is it!" I said.

"Please, please, please, oh, pleasepleasepleaseplease!" Dawn said.

"Do it! Do it!"

"He's opening his mouth!"

That big mouth of Myron's seemed to stay open for about an hour, poised just inches from biting into the sandwich. It was torture!

"Bite!" I hissed.

"Bite!" Dawn said. "Bite it, you . . ."

I tried not to stare, because I didn't want Myron to sense any trouble. But I couldn't help it. See, the frog's head was poking right out between the pieces of bread. It looked like it was staring into Myron's open mouth.

Then . . . Myron bit!

"Yes!"

"Yes!"

Dawn and I high-fived each other.

Myron took a big bite of frog.

Chew, chew, chew.

Then, to my amazement, he took a second bite.

Chew, chew, chew.

A third bite.

And that was when he noticed something was wrong.

FIVE

"*AAAAAAAAAAAAAAARRRRRR GGGGGGGHHHHHH!*"

Myron leapt up.

Myron ripped off the top piece of bread on his sandwich.

Myron took a good long look at what was there, staring with big goggle eyes.

Then he screamed again.

"*AAAAAAAAARRRRRRRGGGGGGGGHH-HHH!*"

By now people were looking. As in, everyone in the lunchroom, all four hundred kids, had stopped eating, stopped talking, and were staring at Myron.

"I . . . ate . . . a . . . FROG!" he cried.

Already I could see the gack dance beginning.

His throat kind of spazzed. His stomach did a kind of wavy thing. His knees looked like they were rattling.

"Gack dance!" Dawn warned me.

"Major gack dance," I agreed. "I estimate three seconds to launch!"

I guess we weren't the only ones who could see what was coming.

"He's gonna chuck!" someone screamed.

"Myron's gonna magoo!" someone else yelled.

The kids nearest to him tried to run.

Too late! There was no escape!

"Buh-BLEAAAAAAH!"

Myron launched a vomit stream that erupted from his mouth like a fire hose.

"It's a force-eight barficane!" Dawn cried.

"Incoming!" I yelled. "Take cover!"

Gumbo sprayed ten feet. It hit one girl so hard she went down, knocked flat on her back by the power of the guttal explosion.

"He's gonna fire again!" I yelled.

"Hugh-hugh-BLEEAAAAAAHHHH!"

Screams! Panic! Desperate kids climbed over each other trying to escape the shower of stomach contents.

It was a scene straight out of Dante's *Inferno!* Or maybe a Jim Carrey movie!

Even Dawn and I had to back away.

But then the eruption seemed to subside. Myron stood perfectly still. He was pale. His eyes were as big as plates. He stared into space.

And then he started to vibrate. He started to rattle. It was like there was an earthquake inside him. It was like he'd swallowed a volcano that was starting to erupt.

"Oh no," I whispered in horror. "He's not done. He's got another one coming! He's NOT DONE! RUN! RUN!"

But our path was blocked by kids too dumb to know that disaster was fast approaching. See, they didn't know what was happening.

It was a very rare phenomenon. Everyone knows the gack dance. Everyone can see that coming.

But this was beyond the gack dance we all knew.

This was . . . the dreaded rocket rawlf!

This was a guttal explosion measured in multitudes.

This was a force ten!

"Hugh-hugh-gug-gugck-BUH-BUH-BUH-BLEEEEEEAAAAAAHHH!"

A huge stream of steaming hot gumbo erupted from Myron. It shot through the air.

And there, right at the front of that deadly barfoleum, was something green.

A frog's head.

It still had a kind of casual expression.

It was just at the tip of the mighty river of puke. It was riding the stream like some kind of deranged surfer.

This was too much for a lot of the kids.

I had read about universal hufferage in books. But I'd never been in the middle of it.

It was horrible! Everywhere kids were launching. It would come in waves, three or four kids at a time, building to more and more as dozens fired simultaneous gut geysers.

It was a tornado of heave!

The floor ran deep with it!

It sloshed around our ankles like runny oatmeal!

It was really quite an unpleasant experience all the way around.

But in the middle of this nightmare scene I realized Dawn was no longer by my side.

I looked for her and saw her walking slowly, like she was in a trance.

She walked, unstoppable, unafraid, through the magoo monsoon toward Myron.

I've never seen anything more foolish. Or braver.

Myron was drained. He was shattered. He could only stare helplessly as Dawn stopped, just a few inches away from him.

She held out her hand, palm down.

Myron's eyes were drawn irresistibly down to that hand. He couldn't look away!

Slowly Dawn turned her hand over.

Myron looked down into the glassy eyes of Frieda Garcia. You could see him trying to figure out what it meant.

Then the memory dawned in his sickly eyes.

Dawn grinned a fierce grin.

"Frieda has had her revenge!" Dawn said.

It was definitely scary. Dawn can be one freaky girl when you make her mad.

And yet I decided right then I really did like her.

SIX

Revenge is sweet.
Unfortunately, revenge never ends.

I mean, Dawn and I got revenge on Myron, right? But now Myron was the one who would be wanting revenge. I knew this. But at the same time I hoped maybe he would just let it go.

The next day I was out walking Heidi and Gretchen. Heidi is a Labrador retriever and Gretchen is a big, bouncy mutt. They're very cool dogs, and their owners are cool too. They never give me any trouble, and they always pay me right on time.

Paying on time is very important.

So, anyway, I was out walking Heidi and

35

Gretchen when I saw Dawn walking along the far side of the street. She was carrying a small grocery bag.

"Hi, Dawn," I called over to her.

She crossed the street. "Hi, Albert. What's up? Are those your dogs?"

"No, I'm a dog walker. It's kind of like my job. I take people's dogs for walks."

"That sounds like fun," she said.

"Not always," I said. "I mean, I have some customers who are totally crazy."

I told her about Mrs. Vernaglia.

"I don't know why you would even put up with that kind of treatment," Dawn said.

I shrugged. "For money. Duh."

We headed toward the park. As we walked, the two dogs seemed to pay a lot of attention to Dawn. Or at least to her bag.

"What's in the bag?"

"Oh, it's just some stuff I picked up for my dad at the deli. Hamburger. Bread. Tongue."

I wrinkled my nose. "Tongue?"

"Beef tongue," Dawn said. "My dad loves it."

I nodded. "I've seen it in the deli. I always

36

wondered whether anyone actually ate that stuff."

"It is kind of creepy," Dawn said. "I mean, it's just this big tongue. It's like the size of one of Shaquille O'Neal's sneakers."

So then we started talking about basketball.

It was a really nice afternoon. The sky was bright, with not too many clouds. The park was full of people playing Frisbee, lying out on blankets, or going through the trash looking for cans.

Just another perfect day in the big city.

At first I didn't even see the danger. I felt it. It was like a chill that went up the back of my neck.

I stopped walking.

"What's the matter?" Dawn demanded.

I shook my head. "I don't know. I just had a sudden feeling of . . . of evil!"

Dawn's eyes went wide. "Myron? Biff?"

"Yes," I said.

We both looked wildly around. Then I spotted them. They were in the shadows, over by a stand of trees.

Myron and Biff.

I met Myron's gaze. He always looked creepy. But this day he was way past creepy. He had the look of an insane ax murderer. Give the boy a hockey mask and you'd have Jason. Give him some long fingernails and you'd have Freddy Kreuger.

Or is it the other way around? I can never keep those ax-murdering lunatics straight.

All I know is, Myron looked like he'd lost it.

"Uh-oh," I said.

Dawn nodded. "Can Heidi and Gretchen beat Biff?"

"I doubt it. They're both pretty smart. I think they'll probably just run."

The truth was, Heidi and Gretchen had spotted Biff. They were both already looking for a way to slip off without being noticed.

"You're dead meat," Myron said suddenly in his thin, reedy voice. He pushed his glasses up on his nose and glared hard at me. "Get them, Biff! Sic! Sic!"

Biff didn't need to be asked twice. He took off, bounding and leaping toward us, his tongue hanging out of his mouth with a trail of slobber flying behind him like the vapor trail of a jet.

"Ahhhh!" I yelled.

"Ooooh!" Dawn cried.

I could feel my feet starting to run. But then something clicked in my terrified brain.

Dead meat.

Slobbery tongue.

Yes! It just might work.

"Give me that beef tongue!" I yelled.

Dawn was quick. She yanked a surprisingly large package from her bag. I swear it weighed ten pounds.

"Okay, I'll lead him off," I said. "You keep the hamburger. Do what you can!"

Then I bailed. I did a Road Runner. You know, where his feet start moving and it kicks up a foot tornado even before his body moves? It was kind of like that.

I tore. I hauled. I ran like all the hounds of heck were after me, even though it was only the one heck-hound.

Biff came for me. And he was faster than I was.

"Rrrraaawrr! Rawarr! Rrrraawwrr!"

I ran, but he gained on me. I could practically smell his deadly dog breath. I could hear his teeth snapping just inches from me.

"Not another pair of jeans!" I moaned. "Mom is going to kill me."

It was time to try my last desperate measure.

I unwrapped the beef tongue as I ran. I tore the white paper away. I littered.

I gripped the tongue in my hand. If you've never seen beef tongue, maybe you're thinking it isn't like an actual tongue. You'd be wrong. It is a tongue. It looks like a tongue. It feels like a tongue, only cold.

I raced at full speed toward a very big, very thick, very tall tree.

It may have been an oak. I don't know. I'm no good at trees. It was big, that's all I cared about.

This would take nerves of steel.

Inches from the tree I suddenly stopped.

I turned to face the rampaging slobber beast.

I held the tongue out in my right hand. I held it out just inches from the tree trunk.

Biff had a choice. He could go for me. Or he could go for the beef tongue.

Biff leapt.

"RRRRAAAWWWRRR RAWRAAAWW-WAAARRR!"

It was scary seeing that horse-size dog leap, let me tell you. Nothing that big should be able to leap through the air and sail that far.

It was unnatural.

That huge, tooth-filled, slobbering dog face came hurtling toward me.

Then his dog nostrils caught the scent of beef tongue.

"Rrrrawwrr? Rawr? RRRRAAAWWWR!"

He shifted direction in midair. He veered to his left. (That would be my right, if you care.)

He hit the tongue with full force.

And a split second later he hit the tree trunk.

SEVEN

BLAMPH!
     Two hundred pounds of flying dog hit the tree. The impact was only softened by the huge beef tongue. The impact chopped the tongue in two. The pointy end went flying and slapped me alongside the head.

Biff lay on the ground, stunned.

I wiped tongue goo off my ear.

Heidi and Gretchen decided this would be an excellent time to steal the beef tongue. They darted in, each grabbed a piece, and retreated to a safe distance.

Slowly, groggily, Biff climbed to his feet.

But then a desperate scream pricked up his ears.

"Biff! Help me, Biff!"

I looked and there, across the meadow, were Myron and Dawn.

Dawn had him down on the ground. She was sitting on his chest. She seemed to be smearing something on him.

Biff raced to protect his master. But he was still unsteady. You could tell by the way he wobbled as he ran.

"Dawn! Look out! Here he comes!" I yelled.

Dawn jumped up and stepped several feet back from Myron.

Myron climbed to his feet, but he looked horrible. He looked red. Like something from the *X-Files*. Like he was smeared with gore.

Suddenly I knew what it was.

Hamburger!

Dawn had smeared Myron with the hamburger. And now Biff, groggy and wobbly but still hungry for beef, was bounding forward.

About halfway to Myron, Biff seemed to change. Suddenly he wasn't racing to save his master. Now he was sniffing the air as he ran. His drool output doubled.

It was right about then that Myron started looking worried.

"Biff! No! It's me!" Myron cried. "It's meeeee!"

But I don't think Biff cared. Biff smelled meat. And after losing that tongue, he was looking for a replacement meal.

See, as a professional dog walker I can tell you something about dogs. Dogs judge everything by how it smells. And Myron smelled like hamburger.

Extra lean.

"Noooooooo!" Myron wailed.

And then Myron started running. Which just made matters worse. Because now in Biff's not-exactly-bright and very groggy brain, Myron was just a big hamburger trying to escape.

"NOOOOOOOOOO!" Myron screamed.

Biff bounded after him as Myron ran for his life.

They disappeared behind some trees.

I trotted over to where Dawn stood. "I almost feel sorry for the guy," I said.

"Me too," she said.

Then we looked at each other and started giggling. "Yeah, right," I said.

"As if," Dawn agreed.

"That was smart of you to hamburger Myron," I said.

"And that was brilliant the way you matadored Biff with the tongue."

"I have to go pick up Princess at Mrs. Vernaglia's now. Do . . . um . . . I mean, do you want to hang out some more?"

"I'd love to," Dawn said.

I felt a little queasy from the way she looked at me. But it was a good kind of nausea.

It was a kind of perfect moment.

Except for the fact that in the distance I could hear Myron's shrill voice screaming, "I'll get you, Albert! I'll get you booooooooth. Ahhhh! NO! Down, boy! Dooooowwwwn!"

EIGHT

"Worms!" Mrs. Vernaglia yelled as I walked into her bedroom.

I jumped about four inches straight up.

"Worms! My little Princess has worms!"

Dawn had walked with me over to Mrs. Vernaglia's building, so she was with me when I went in to pick up Princess.

I expected it to be no big deal. I mean, I picked Princess up for her walk every afternoon. But suddenly, as soon as Dawn and I walked through the door, Mrs. Vernaglia had just totally gone off.

"Mrs. Vernaglia, what are you saying?" I asked, as politely and calmly as I could. I mean, my nerves were already pretty shaky after the close call in the park with Myron and Biff.

"Princess was scooting her bottom over the rug," Mrs. Vernaglia shrieked. "So I called an ambulance and took her to the veterinarian."

"You called an ambulance because your dog had an itchy heiny?" Dawn asked in disbelief.

Mrs. Vernaglia glared at Dawn like she had just noticed her being there. "Of course. I couldn't allow my baby to suffer."

"She'll be okay, though, right?" I asked.

Mrs. Vernaglia hugged the little rat dog against her. The incredible diamond collar glittered so brightly I had to squint. "She is traumatized. As soon as I come back from the hospital I'll call in the finest dog psychologists. Princess has never had *anything* wrong with her. Let alone worms!"

"Mrs. Vernaglia, a lot of dogs get worms. It's very common."

That was a mistake. I knew as soon as I said it I should not have used the word *common* in relation to Princess.

Mrs. Vernaglia's mouth snapped open so fast, I was afraid her dentures might slip again.

"Common? Common? I'll have you know this is no ordinary case of worms. Princess has a very rare case. The doctor said it was a parasite from South America. Possibly Brazil."

She calmed down a little. "Fortunately there is a medicine. I will give it to her tomorrow morning just before I leave for the hospital. The veterinarian said that she would pass the worms sometime within twelve hours of taking the medicine."

"Excuse me?" I asked. "Pass the worms? What does that mean?"

"Why, they will come out with her deposit." She paused to consider. "You must be *sure* to save that deposit for me so that I can check it when I get back. To be sure that Princess is better."

I felt a wave of nausea sweeping over me. I have to confess something. I have a pretty strong stomach, but I really, really can't stand worms. Any kind of worms. Let alone worms that live inside dogs or cats or people.

Worms should be in the ground, in my opinion. They should not be inside living animals.

It all goes back to my childhood. Like years ago.

Flashback . . . flashback. . . flashback . . .

It was my birthday.

I had a party with all my friends. You know, cake, ice cream, the whole deal. They all brought presents and that was cool and all. But you know how it is with presents. Sometimes they just don't seem all that great. Like when your aunt buys you underwear. Or one of your friends gives you some action figures that aren't wrapped in their original package and look like maybe they've already been played with for a couple of weeks.

Still, you're grateful people bought you stuff. It's always better to have *more* stuff, even if it isn't *great* stuff.

But when the party was over, I felt a little down. A little melancholy.

Maybe because I realized that life never lives up to the ideal and that wanting is better than having.

Or maybe I was just sick from gorging down half a birthday cake and a few pints of ice cream. Plus candy.

Anyway, all my friends finally left. And it was then that my mom and dad brought me a special box. It had air holes poked in it.

"What is it?" I wondered with childish curiosity.

"Open it and see," my dad said, grinning down at me.

My mom hugged him around the waist and the two of them beamed at me.

"We know how you love animals," my mom said.

Animals? Had they gotten me a pet at long last? Oh, please, oh, please! I thought.

I tore off the wrapping.

I lifted off the lid.

In the box was a cute, fluffy little kitten. He was an orange tabby with blue eyes.

"Mom! Dad!" I cried. "You got me a kitty!"

"Yes, son, we know you've wanted a pet for a long time."

I lifted the little kitten up out of the box. "I'm going to name him Power Ranger," I said.

My parents looked a little unsure about that, but it was my kitten, after all.

I held him high in my hands and danced around in innocent glee.

I'll admit, Power Ranger looked just a little sick. But I didn't care right then, because I was just so happy.

"Mew," he said in a tiny little voice.

I held him up over my head. And I said, "I'll love him forever!"

And just at that moment was when he did it.

Splurt!

He popped like an upside-down volcano.

Litter loaf.

Garfield goo.

The fifth regrettable fluid. The liquid brown substance.

Splurt!

It landed with a series of sickening plops right on my face. And let's face it, that would have been bad enough. But I already had a little baby brother, so I was pretty well used to heinous acts of hinder production.

But this was different.

"*Aaaiiieeee!*" I screamed.

In panic I threw Power Ranger through the air. He landed on the La-Z-Boy. I raced for the bathroom to wash off the pooptonium.

I lurched to the sink, clutching the cold porcelain for comfort. And then I stared in horror at the reflection in the mirror.

Yes, I had been used like a litter box. Yes, there was used Iams dribbling sluggishly down my face.

But that wasn't the true horror.

See, the brown substance was . . . alive!

ALIVE!

Wriggling, curling, uncurling worms!

WORMS!

NINE

"WORMS!" I screamed. "WORMS! Get them off me!"

Mrs. Vernaglia stopped talking and stared at me. Dawn was edging away, like maybe I was dangerously crazy and she wanted some distance.

"Sorry," I said shakily. "I was in a flashback."

Mrs. Vernaglia and Dawn both nodded.

"Oh, okay," Mrs. Vernaglia said. She went back to yammering about Princess.

I mopped my brow and tried to pay attention. But the memory of the terrible Power Ranger incident still made me want to run and wash my face.

By the way, Power Ranger was fine. He

weighs as much as a Thanksgiving turkey now. He spends his days sitting in the sun, eating, clawing holes in the carpet, eating, trying to find a way to escape from our apartment, and eating.

But sometimes I think maybe the Power Ranger incident is part of the reason why I prefer dogs now.

"Here is the key to this apartment," Mrs. Vernaglia said. She handed me a key. "Tomorrow you will be in complete charge of Princess. And I want to see *each* of her deposits."

"Yes, ma'am," I said, taking the key.

"Now, go ahead and take her out."

"Yes, ma'am. Just let me take this diamond collar off her and—"

"What?" Mrs. Vernaglia shrieked.

"I'm just going to unfasten her collar and leave it here. After all, it cost a fortune and—"

"You'll do no such thing!" Mrs. Vernaglia snapped. "Princess must have her necklace. Don't you see her cute little name tag with her home address and phone number and the phone number of my lawyer? What if something terrible should happen? What if you were run over by a bus and Princess ran away? I might never find her again."

I was feeling a little panicky. I guess I figured she'd change her mind about the collar. "But Mrs. Vernaglia, this is the big city. You can't have a little dog running around with a fortune in diamonds . . . I mean, look, it's dangerous out there."

"A princess must dress like a princess," Mrs. Vernaglia said, looking very haughty.

"What, are you NUTS?" I yelled. "You're going to get me killed, you crazy woman. Forget it! You can walk your own rat dog, and good riddance to both of you!"

Okay, maybe that's not *exactly* what I said. What I really said was, "Okay."

"If I learn that you have let Princess go out without her necklace," Mrs. Vernaglia said, "I won't pay you a dime of that hundred dollars. And don't forget: I have many friends in the neighborhood."

I doubted that.

"Yes, Mrs. Vernaglia," I said. I took Princess from her arms and fastened the leash to her diamond collar.

Outside on the street Dawn said, "That lady is slightly crazy, isn't she?"

"Slightly?"

Princess began yip-yip-yipping.

"Well, at least we won't have Myron and Biff to worry about. I think Myron has had it for today."

"Probably," I said glumly. "But he's going to want revenge more than ever. Plus now I have more to worry about than Myron."

Dawn smiled at me. "How about if I help you? I'm not doing anything this weekend."

"I'm not giving you any of the money!" I snapped.

Dawn rolled her eyes. "Is money all you care about?"

"Sure. What else is there?"

"Someday you'll find out," she said.

Yeah, right, I thought. Like anything could be more important than money.

Princess stopped near a tree and began doing her business. I tried not to think of the big, juicy worm that was just waiting for the medicine to make it appear.

"I guess I'll meet you at Mrs. Vernaglia's

apartment tomorrow," I said to Dawn.

"It's a date," Dawn said, smiling sweetly.

"Yip! Yip! Yip!" Princess said.

At that moment I guess I felt like the whole world was in my hands. I would soon have a hundred dollars to add to my bank account. Plus Dawn would help me with Princess for nothing!

Little did I know that I was perched on the very threshold of total disaster.

TEN

Saturday. The day I would make a hundred bucks in a single day. The greatest day of my life so far. Even better than the day I found a ten-dollar bill on the subway.

I met Dawn outside Mrs. Vernaglia's building. We took the elevator up together. I used the key to let me in.

"Kind of creepy in here with Mrs. Vernaglia gone," Dawn said.

"It's pretty creepy with her here too," I said.

"Yip! Yip! Yip!"

Princess came scampering out of Mrs. Vernaglia's bedroom. She was wearing the diamond collar.

"There's a note," Dawn said. She pointed to a piece of paper lying on Mrs. Vernaglia's dresser.

I picked it up and read it. "It's a reminder to save all Princess's deposits. Especially the one with the worm. Princess took her medicine this morning."

I looked at the little dog with even less affection than usual. Princess has never been anything but an annoying little rat dog. But thinking of her with a worm coiled up inside her . . . well, it didn't make me like her any more.

"Come on, Princess. Time for your walk."

"Yip! Yip! Yip!"

I snapped on the leash. We headed outside. Me and Dawn and Princess and that stupid collar.

The day before no one had seemed to take much notice of Princess's collar. But that was a Friday and everyone was rushing around. This was Saturday. The park was full of people. People having picnics. People playing music. People playing softball.

The park was as busy as a shopping mall.

And a lot of those people paid attention to Princess's collar. People walking by would stop and stare. People throwing Frisbees would become distracted and get hit in the ear by their Frisbees.

People were definitely noticing.

"Yip! Yip! Yip!" Princess kept up her usual annoying barking, which just drew even more attention.

And that was why I decided we should get away from the crowds, get off the main paths and try to find some privacy.

Looking back on it all now, it was maybe not such a great idea.

"Let's head into the trees a little," I said to Dawn.

So we did. Back into the trees. Out of sight of most of the people in the park.

We walked over crunchy fallen leaves. We scraped through bushes. We got the leash tangled in the undergrowth.

And the whole time I had this weird feeling. Like the hairs on the back of my head were standing up. I felt like someone was watching us.

At last we found ourselves near a high embankment. Like a hill, basically. Up at the top of the hill was part of a jogging path. I could see people running by, listening to headphones.

Just ahead of us we could see a big drainage pipe that went into the side of the embankment. I looked around, but I couldn't see anyone.

"This is kind of a gross place," Dawn said. "Maybe we should get back to the meadow."

I nodded. "Yeah. I wanted privacy, but this is too much."

"Yip! Yip! Yip! Yipyipyipyipyip!"

"What's the matter with the dog?" Dawn asked.

"Probably nothing," I said. But I was getting worried. I know Princess's usual yipping. This was *unusual* yipping.

"Maybe it's like Lassie, and she's trying to warn us of something," Dawn said.

"Yip! Yip! Yipyipyipyipyipyip!"

"This is much more excited than she usually is," I said.

Then suddenly I saw the reason why.

They had been hiding behind a tree: Myron and Biff.

I nudged Dawn and pointed.

"Uh-oh," she said. "Not again."

"Hi, Myron," I sneered, hoping I sounded tough and unafraid.

"Hello, Albert," he said. "Hello, Dawn. The time has come at last. You don't have any deli food this time. No hamburger, no beef tongue, not even a salami. You're defenseless."

I swallowed. I looked around. We were trapped. There was nowhere to run.

"And guess what?" Myron said, grinning an evil grin. "I haven't fed Biff anything since yesterday. He's very hungry. And when he gets hungry, he gets mean."

"Myron, you better not—" I started to say.

"Get 'em, Biff! Get 'em. For the final time, sic! Finish them off!"

Biff, that dog in the shape of a mountain, came rumbling toward us, tongue lolling, slobber flying, teeth bare and yellow.

We couldn't run left. The trees and bushes were too thick. Biff would catch us. We couldn't run up the embankment—it was too steep.

There was only one way.

"Into the drainpipe!" I yelled.

ELEVEN

I ran. Dawn ran. Even Princess ran, yip-yip-yipping as she scampered on her tiny little legs.

We raced for the gaping black hole of the drainpipe.

"Raawwrrr! Rawwwrrrr! RRAAWWRRR!"

Biff was just twenty feet back and catching up.

Into the pipe! Into the gaping maw!

It was about six feet in diameter. Plenty big for us. It was hard to run because it was corrugated metal and round, so we kind of stumbled at first. But we noticed this slowed Biff down too. I yanked Princess up into my arms and held her so we could run faster.

She instantly unloaded on me. But that was the least of my worries.

There was water sloshing around our feet. At least I hoped it was water and not something much worse.

There was a foul smell of rot and mildew and fungus. And other things I didn't want to think about.

It got darker and darker the farther we went. Soon we could barely see anything. But we could still hear.

"Raawwrrr! Rawrrr! Rrrrraawwr!"

To which Princess answered, "Yip! Yip! Yip!"

We were losing the battle of the barking. And Biff wasn't giving up.

On and on we ran. Deeper and deeper. We had run a couple of blocks at least. Maybe more. It's hard to tell. The only light was an occasional dim shaft of sunlight that seemed to come from far above. But for long periods we were almost blind.

"I . . . I . . . can't run anymore," Dawn gasped.

"We . . . have to . . . go on," I said.

But the truth was, I knew I was too tired. I would have to stop running soon. This time Biff would catch us!

"There's . . . a turn . . . a side tunnel!" Dawn cried.

"Take it!"

We turned right into a slightly smaller pipe. Now we could almost feel the pipe scraping the tops of our heads.

"Raawwwr! Rawwwr! Rrrrawwr!"

"He's still with us! But there's another turn!"

I don't remember how many turns we took. Several. Too many to keep track of.

We were deep in the sewer system of the city. And the smell was getting worse with every step.

"The stench!" Dawn cried. "I may have to hurl!"

"Don't chuck," I cried. "It will slow us down!"

Suddenly, without any warning, the pipe changed. It was no longer metal. It was bricks. A round, brick pipe. In the dim light I could see that the walls were covered with slime.

Things were growing down there. Things that might not even have names.

"Rawrrr! Rrrrrawwr! Raawwr!"

"I can't go on!" Dawn wailed.

"Hang on, Dawn," I yelled.

"Yip! Yip! Yip!"

There was another problem now. The water was deeper. It was up around our knees and getting deeper. We splashed along through the dark foul water in a nightmare of growing stench.

Then I saw a log in the water. At last! Something I could use against Biff!

"Stop! We're gonna fight it out!"

Dawn stopped, exhausted. I handed Princess to her.

"How are you going to do that?" she demanded.

"I'm going to slam Biff with this floating log," I said. I grabbed on to the back of the log. It felt strange. Not exactly like a log. It was bumpy. Bumpy and kind of flexible. And it wasn't a log shape, really. It tapered down to a point at the back.

Then through the dark I spotted Biff. His

red eyes glittered. His yellow teeth shone.

I waited till just the right moment. Then, with a mighty shove, I shot the log toward him.

That was when the log opened its jaw.

"Hchchhhhaaaahhhssss!"

"ROWR?!"

"Yip?"

"What?"

"Aaaahhhhhh! It's an ALLIGATOR!"

It was definitely an alligator. It may have looked like a floating log, but now I knew why it felt all knobby. I had been holding on to the tail of an alligator that was probably twenty feet long.

The alligator snapped at Biff.

Then he turned and opened his huge, powerful jaws and snapped at us.

Biff went one way. We went the other. Suddenly no one was tired.

I ran so fast, I think I actually ran *on* water.

We took more turns and more twists and finally collapsed in a section of pipe that was fairly dry.

We flopped down to the ground and just panted for a while.

"I think we lost the gator," I said.

"We lost Biff too," Dawn said.

"There's just one little problem," I said. "We also lost ourselves. We are lost deep in the sewers of the city. Lost in a world of stench and filth and regrettable fluids!"

TWELVE

"I thought all those stories about there being alligators in the sewers were just dumb stories," Dawn said.

"Guess not."

"So now where do we go?"

"Anywhere except back there," I said. I leaned against the side of the pipe.

Big mistake.

"Yargh!" I cried. My hand had sunk four inches into black-and-green slime.

"This is the grossest place on earth," Dawn said. "It's so slimy, it's like we're trapped in some giant's snotty nostril."

"This is like the home office of the five regrettable fluids," I said. "Mucus, pukus, waximus auriculas, numero uno, and numero dos."

Dawn looked at me with surprised respect. "I didn't know you were so smart. You know the five regrettable fluids in the original Latin? I only know them in English: snot, puke, earwax, squirt, and number two. It sounds so much more romantic in Latin."

I shrugged. "I figure you have to get an education if you want to get rich."

She sighed. "And that's what really matters to you, isn't it?"

"Yeah. What else would matter?"

"How about friendship?"

The way she said it made me uncomfortable. "Yeah, friendship is important too."

"You don't sound like you mean it. Let me put it this way, Albert. The other day I helped you get revenge on Myron with the frogwich. And then I helped save you by applying the raw hamburger facial."

"Uh-huh," I said.

"And now I'm down here with you again. Now, which would you rather have down here in the sewer with you? Me or a twenty-dollar bill?"

This was a very complicated question. On the one hand, twenty dollars wouldn't help me much down here. On the other hand, twenty dollars was still twenty dollars. . . .

I guess Dawn got tired of waiting for me to come up with an answer. "Oh, forget it," she snapped. "But someday you're going to learn. Money isn't everything. There's also friendship. And loyalty. And dignity."

"And revenge," I added, picturing her with the head of Frieda Garcia.

"Well, okay, revenge is cool too."

There was a stream of water running right down the bottom of the pipe. It was dirty runoff from the streets above. It gurgled around thrown-away shoes and used foam cups and cans.

There was light from above. It came from long shafts that went up to the street. These were sewer drains in the curbs up above. I could even hear the sounds of traffic from up there. I stood on tiptoe and saw a flash of yellow taxi cabs.

"We have to find a way out of here," Dawn said.

"Mrs. Vernaglia would kill me if she knew where I had her Princess," I said glumly.

"Um, Albert?"

"Yeah?"

"Where is Princess?"

My heart stopped. I mean, it really stopped. For like five seconds I think I was dead. Then it beat again.

"PRINCESS!"

I jumped straight up. My head hit the scummy, slimy top of the pipe. For a second I was glued in place. Then I fell back down.

"Where is Princess?" I yelled.

Dawn shrugged helplessly. "I don't know. I thought *you* had her."

"The alligator. The alligator ate her!" I moaned.

"No, no, I saw her in your arms *after* we got away from the alligator."

"We have to find her," I said. "Oh no. Oh no. She's wearing that stupid diamond collar. Oh, I am dead. I am so dead."

Then, far off, I heard it. "Yip! Yip! Yip!"

"That's her! That's the little rat dog's voice! It was coming from down there." I pointed

73

farther down the dark, stinking tunnel. "Princess! Princess! Come back, girl! Come back!"

We took off down the sewer pipe at a sloshing, slipping run.

"Princess!"

"Princess!"

Suddenly I remembered. "Wait! We have to keep an eye out."

"For what?"

"For Princess's deposits. If I don't show Mrs. Vernaglia her wormy deposit, I won't get paid."

"Albert, how are we going to see a Chihuahua chunk down here in all this filth and slime?"

"Well, if Mrs. Vernaglia is right, it will be *moving*. That should help."

We slowed to a trot and kept a sharp eye out for Princess's dog bars.

"Oh, man," Dawn groaned suddenly. "What is that smell? It's awful. It's heinous!"

She was not exaggerating. I've smelled some deadly smells. I've smelled diaper gravy. I've smelled the dead things some of the dogs like to bring me. I've smelled bus stations.

But this! This was the true nose killer.

"I can't go on," Dawn said. "That . . . that odor! That evil aroma! It's morbific!"

The stench was like a wall, blocking our path. It was like a physical force. Like a force field on *Star Trek*.

"We . . . must . . . go on," I gagged.

"I'll hurl if I go any closer," Dawn cried. "I'm already doing the warm-up exercises for the gack dance!"

Then to our ears came a faint, "Yip! Yip! Yip!"

"Must . . . go on," I said. I leaned forward, fighting the awesome power of the stench. I looked over to see Dawn keeping pace with me. But she was definitely loading up for a launch. Her throat was doing the gack dance. Her stomach was wiffling like a flag on a windy day.

Then we saw the pile. It was illuminated by a shaft of light from the street above.

The pile was probably three feet high. At the top the pile was sort of washed-out red in color. At the bottom it was brown. Here and there were splashes of yellow.

"That's where . . . the stench is coming from," I managed to say. "If we can just . . . get . . . past it!"

But now the stench was coming at us in waves. Odor waves battered me back like a strong wind.

Now I was doing the gack dance too. I was doing the whole puke polka!

Then suddenly, as I got closer, I realized what the pile was.

"Hot dogs!" I gasped. "There must be hundreds! Thousands!"

In a flash I knew what had happened. The hot dog vendor on the street above must be dumping his leftover hot dogs down the sewer each night. He must have been doing it for years!

It was a three-foot-tall pile of rotting, burst, decomposed hot dogs. Hot dogs growing mildew. Hot dogs growing fungus. Hot dogs growing moss. Hot dogs oozing some mysterious liquid.

And mixed through the hot dogs of death: sauerkraut!

"No! No!" I cried. "Not sauerkraut!"

I hate sauerkraut.

Still, I knew we had to go on. For Princess. For Princess's collar. And because if we went back the other way, we'd run into that alligator.

"We have to get past the hot dogs," I said to Dawn. She didn't answer. Possibly because she really didn't want to open her mouth right then.

I took her hand and pulled her forward.

Squich!

A rotting hot dog burst open under my foot.

Squich! Squich!

We began to climb the hot dog hill. And then, a quarter of the way through that living nightmare of rot and reek, I noticed something.

Hot Dog Hill was alive.

Alive!

ALIVE!

THIRTEEN

"**D**awn!" I whispered. "The hot dogs are . . . moving!"

I looked down to see my feet, sunk in a mire of new and old frankfurters.

There were pale, wormy strands of sauerkraut wrapped around my ankles. It was *rotten* sauerkraut, not fresh. Like there's a difference.

And there, in the putrid meat, they crawled. The roaches.

Thousands of cockroaches.

Thousands of *big* cockroaches.

"*AAAAAAHHHHHHH!*" Dawn screamed.

"*AAAAAAHHHHHHH!*" I agreed.

We started to run. But the goo of decayed meat held our feet like molasses.

Cockroaches began scurrying up our legs.

"*NOOOOOOOOOOOOOO!*"

"*NOOOOOOOOOOOOOOO!*"

Streams of roaches scrabbled up my jeans. I tried to run. I could barely move.

Then through wide, panicked eyes, I saw the others. They covered the walls of the sewer like a bad coat of paint. Their gleaming brown wings caught the dim light from the street above. Millions of bug antennae waved at us.

Millions of cockroaches. They were everywhere! They were ahead of us and behind. They were coming closer. Like . . . like they expected something. Like they were waiting for something. Like . . .

Sploooosh! Plop! Plop! Plopploploplop!

Down the shaft from the street above they fell. Hot and fragrant. Hot dogs! Fresh hot dogs!

Or as fresh as street vendor hot dogs ever get.

"Ow!" Dawn cried as a hot one slapped her cheek.

"That's why the roaches are coming! It's feeding time!"

The shower of hot dogs fell all around us. Then . . .

Splurp.

"I know that sound!" I cried. "It's the sound of sauerkraut sliding down the—"

It hit me right on the head. A huge mound of prerotten cabbage.

At that very instant the roaches launched themselves at the food. Billions of little legs scrabbled all together, making a noise I will never forget.

"RUN!" I screamed at Dawn.

But Dawn had reached her limit. *"Guh-guh-BLEAH!"*

Dawn fired her lunch missile. She did the blew magoo. Steaming hot gumbo exploded from her mouth in a violent stream.

I think I saw her actual pancreas go flying past!

She was huffing up her internal organs!

It was a force-ten barficane! A force ten, I tell you! And it was aimed right at me!

I couldn't exactly blame her. But I didn't like it either.

What happened next, I . . . I can't even describe. It was beyond description.

Okay, I'll try to describe it.

Vomit filled the air.

There was bad meat in my shoes.

Roaches rushed like an army. Other roaches were already crawling up my pant legs.

Sauerkraut dribbled down my head.

And everywhere was the awesome stench of rotting meat and meat by-products.

The horror!

The horror!

I threw back my head and shook my fist at fate. "Why?" I cried. "Why? WHY?"

And as an answer fate dropped another load of sauerkraut on my upturned face.

FOURTEEN

I was not a happy person. Neither was Dawn. It seemed to take forever to get free of the hot dog hill of death. But at last we were away from it, running over a crawling carpet of cockroaches.

Crunch, crunch, crunch.

At last we made it away from the cockroaches. Our footsteps went from *crunch* to *squish* again.

"Sorry I blew stomach contents all over you," Dawn said sheepishly.

"That's okay," I said. "I was already covered in sauerkraut."

"These shoes are ruined," Dawn said, looking down at her sneakers, which were a mass of slime, hot dog bits, dead roaches, and assorted goo.

"I could use a shower," I said. "I mean, I could really, really use a shower."

"Yip! Yip! Yip!"

"That sounded closer," Dawn said hopefully.

"Yeah. Let's go get that stupid dog and find a way out of here."

We trudged along the endless tunnel. The only good thing was that we seemed to be closer to the street now. The shafts leading up to the curbs were shorter. We could hear familiar big city street noises—honking, sirens, gunfire, and cursing.

"Maybe we can get close enough to the surface to yell and get help," Dawn said.

Then we looked at each other and laughed. "Yeah, right. Like anyone in this city would actually stop and listen to someone yelling from the sewer."

The laughter was a relief. It helped me cope a little with the horror of the hot dog hill. Although it would be days before I could bring myself to eat one again.

"Yip! Yip! Yip!"

"That's definitely closer," I said. "Up ahead. There's an intersection. I think it sounds like she's to the left."

We reached the pipe intersection. We could go forward, left, or right. Neither of us was going to go back. We knew what was behind us.

"Yip! Yip! Yip!"

"Definitely left," Dawn said.

"Besides, it looks lighter down there," I said.

Sure enough, we were now closer to the street above, and the sewer pipe was almost bright. In a filthy, dingy sort of way. Unfortunately it was also smaller, so we had to walk hunched over.

"Come here, doggy. Nice doggy. Come here."

Dawn and I froze. We looked at each other. That was definitely a human voice we had heard.

We edged cautiously forward. There, around a bend in the pipe, was Princess. Her diamond collar glittered brilliantly in a shaft of sunlight.

The sunlight came from a sewer drain just a few feet above her. And there, sticking down from the sewer, was an arm. It was reaching for Princess.

I ran forward. "Help! Help!"

The arm pulled back. A face appeared just a few feet away. It was hard to tell, since I don't usually meet people when they are kneeling to look through a sewer drain, but I had the feeling it was not a nice face.

"Help us—we're kind of trapped down here," Dawn said.

The face grinned. Okay, now I was sure: it was not a nice face. It wasn't even a nice arm. For one thing, he had a huge tattoo of Darth Vader. No way was that a good sign.

"Yeah, sure, I'll help you," the face said. "Just give me that doggie collar first."

"The dog collar?" I said. I gulped hard. "You don't want that collar. Those aren't real diamonds, or anything."

"Hey, kid. I'm a professional thief. I know real diamonds when I see them. Give me the collar and I'll get you out."

"I don't think so," I said.

"I'm not *asking*, kid." The face sneered. "I'm *telling*. Give me that mutt's collar or I'm coming in after you!"

"As if," Dawn said with a laugh.

"Yeah, how are you going to come in here after me?" I said.

"There's a manhole right up the street!" he said, grinning viciously. "That's it. You had your chance. I'm gonna get those diamonds!"

With that he disappeared.

"Oh no," I wailed. "I can't let that creep get the collar."

"Why not?" Dawn asked. "What are you going to do? That guy looked big."

"If I lose the collar, I don't get paid!"

"Albert, even you must know that staying alive is more important than money."

"I must? Besides, hey, we're getting scared for nothing. That guy isn't coming down here. Manhole covers weigh too much for one guy to lift them up. Trust me."

Just then, gazing down the long dark pipe, I saw a sudden new shaft of light. A round shaft of light. About the size of a manhole cover.

"Uh-huh. Trust you," Dawn said. "Right."

A pair of legs appeared, climbing down through the manhole.

Big legs. Strong legs. The kind of legs a really big, really strong guy would have.

"Here we go again," I said wearily. "RUN!"

FIFTEEN

"It's getting darker!" Dawn cried as we ran.

"That's because we're going deeper!" I yelled to her.

"Yip! Yip! Yip!"

"I'll get you," the thief shouted. "I'll get you and your little dog too!"

We were deep, deep in the sewer system of the city. The shafts of light were coming from much higher up. We could no longer hear any street sounds. All we could hear was the thief, running after us.

"Just give him the collar! Mrs. Vernaglia can't make you pay for it," Dawn said. "I can't keep running."

"I can't give it to him," I said. "I won't get

my hundred bucks! And I want my hundred bucks!"

So we kept running. Even though the walls of the pipe were growing ever snottier. They were coated with slime. *We* were coated with slime.

"Look! Up ahead!" Dawn said. "Some kind of open area, I think."

"Maybe there will be a way out!"

We slipped and slid and slithered along the slime pipe. Then suddenly we were in a vast open space. It was like some kind of cave, almost. Like a covered swimming pool of sewage.

It was round, probably fifty feet across. Placed around this chamber were six different pipes, each oozing and dribbling liquids you didn't want to think about.

There was a narrow walkway that went around the chamber. But in places the walkway had crumbled and fallen into the pool.

And in the center of the pool was a round platform, all by itself. Not connected to anything.

The pool was black. The color of used

engine oil. Heavy and sloggy like oatmeal.

And there was a smell.

Oh, man, was there a smell.

Fortunately the deadly rotting Hot Dog Hill of Horror had destroyed some of my ability to smell. It would be weeks before I would totally regain my sense of smell, and it would involve the perfume counter at Bloomingdale's. But that's a whole other story.

I'm telling you this: I was glad my sense of smell was damaged. I was glad I could not smell every one of the individual stenches that went to make up that one master reek.

Because even with my nose impaired, it was heinous.

It was morbific.

And it was familiar.

"I know what this is," I whispered. "We have discovered the fabled Chamber of the Five Regrettable Fluids!"

"Say what?"

"It's not very well known," I explained, "but the city sewer system has filters that separate out the five regrettable fluids from everything else. This way each of the five regrettables can be disposed of in its own special way."

"How do you know these things, Albert?"

"Sometimes there is an overflow. At least that's what *they* want you to believe. And then the extra fluids drain off. Into the Chamber of the Five Regrettable Fluids. What we are looking at *is* that chamber."

Over each of the other five pipes was a plaque. Old, ancient plaques with Latin names: Mucus. Pukus. And so on. The pipe labeled Waximus Auriculas was bright orange. It carried two centuries or more of earwax. George Washington's earwax had probably traveled down that pipe.

I stepped out on the narrow catwalk and craned my neck to see the plaque over our pipe. It said, Miscellaneous.

"Ha! I got you now!" the thief yelled as he came into view.

"Quick! We have to go around on the catwalk!" I said.

"But it's crumbling!" Dawn cried.

"We have no choice!"

We started around the chamber on the

narrow ledge. It was barely wide enough for our feet. The only one with enough room to walk was Princess.

"Yip! Yip! Yip!"

"You can't get away!" the thief shouted.

"I'm gonna slip!" Dawn whimpered.

"Come on, hang in there. We're almost to the next pipe! We can escape down the Pukus pipe!"

"Ewww."

"We're going to make it!"

But then something happened that shattered my last hope. Emerging from the Pukus pipe was a beast.

The beast.

Biff!

Biff didn't look too good. And when Myron appeared behind him, he looked even worse. I don't think either of them had an easy trip through the sewers. Myron looked like some bad science fiction movie slime monster.

"You!" Myron cried in a weird voice. "You! This is all your fault! Do you . . . do you . . . do you know what I've been through?" he screamed. "I've been through the bowels of the netherworld! Someone is gonna pay. And it's gonna be YOU!"

This was ahead of us. Behind us was the thief, who looked like an Arnold Schwarzenegger gone seriously rotten.

"Give me the jewels, and maybe I won't hurt you!"

Blocked ahead. Blocked behind.

There was only one way out.

And it involved swimming.

Swimming in two hundred years' worth of regrettable fluids.

SIXTEEN

"We have to swim for it," I said as calmly as I could. "That pipe over there? The Waximus Auriculas pipe? The catwalk is destroyed on either side of it. If we get there, Myron and the thief can't follow us!"

"We'd have to swim this . . . this . . . goo! The five regrettable fluids all united. This is megawad you're talking about! The megawad in liquid form!"

"I know, Dawn. But it's the only way! The ONLY WAY!"

Myron was still ranting and raving. "Now, Biff. Go, Biff! I charge you with a mission of utter destruction! Sic, boy! SIC! Annihilate them both!"

The big huge thief rushed us from the left.
The big huge dog rushed us from the right.
What could we do?
We jumped.
Into the goo. Into the slime. Into the black river of gumbo! Into . . . the megawad!
It wrapped around me. It hugged me with an evil, gooey embrace.
It seeped through my clothes. It filled my pockets and my shoes.
I . . . I don't know if I can talk about it anymore. It was a nightmare. A seemingly endless nightmare of swimming, and swimming, and swimming, and swimming, and SWIMMING, AND SWIMMING, AND—
Okay. Okay, I'm cool.
I'll be okay. Sorry. It's just that for a minute, I was back there. You know what I mean?
It was horror beyond horror. The five regrettable fluids, forming the megawad of viscous product.
It seemed like forever before I reached the far side of the pool. And then I was so out of it, I slammed into the concrete and twisted my wrist.

"Why? Why is this happening to me?" I cried.

"It's okay, Albert. It's okay. We made it!" It was Dawn's sweet voice.

I felt someone drawing me up out of the death goo. I was sitting on the narrow catwalk. I opened my eyes for the first time.

What I saw was Myron and Biff, stuck on the far side of the chamber. They couldn't reach us.

"Nooooo!" Myron cried in frustration. "NOOOO!"

The thief was trapped too, unable to reach us.

"I'll get you!" he yelled.

But his heart wasn't in it. He knew we had escaped.

I had a terrible sinking feeling. Princess!

"Where is Princess?" I shrieked. "I . . . I must have let her go!"

But then I saw Princess. She was dog-paddling through the goo.

Somehow I must have let her go while I was crossing. I wasn't really thinking all that clearly during the swim.

"She's going to make it," Dawn said. "I saw her stop at the platform to rest. But she dived right back in."

"I can't believe it!" I said. I hate to admit it, but I was surprised. I would never have thought the little rat dog had the guts to swim the liquid megawad.

But I guess we never know the limits of courage until we are put to the test. And I guess, despite what I thought of her, Princess had courage.

The plucky little dog reached our side of the pool. With my one good hand I pulled her to safety.

"That was pretty cool, Princess," I said, filled with new respect for her.

"Ruff! Ruff! Ruff!" she said.

"What?" I cried.

"Ruff! Ruff! Ruff!" Princess barked.

Dawn and I both laughed in relief. We had made it! We had survived! The two of us and Princess too. We had survived the most horrible test anyone, human or dog, could ever live through.

"Oh no," Dawn said suddenly.

"What?"

"Look!"

I followed the direction of her outstretched finger. She was pointing at the platform in the middle of the pool.

On that platform was a small mound.

Princess's deposit.

It was moving. It was the wormy deposit.

"Oh no," I moaned. "I . . . I have to have that deposit, or Mrs. Vernaglia will never pay me! After all this! I won't even get paid! I have to . . . to . . . to go back for it."

Dawn put a hand on my shoulder. A slimy, awful hand, but I wasn't one to complain.

"You can't swim," she said. "Your wrist is sprained. You'd never make it."

"Oh no. Nooooo!"

"Albert? I know how important money is to you. If you want me to, I will swim back and collect the deposit."

Wow. There it was. The moment of truth.

If I wanted my money I would have to ask Dawn to reenter the Chamber of the Five Regrettables.

It all came down to this: Was money really

all that mattered to me? Was I willing to make Dawn do a terrible thing just for money?

We had been through so much, Dawn and me. I hoped we would be friends forever.

But if I made her reenter the death gumbo . . . it would probably be over between us.

It was the biggest decision of my life.

SEVENTEEN

"Thanks, Mrs. Vernaglia," I said, counting the five twenty-dollar bills.

It was the next day. Mrs. Vernaglia was back from the hospital. Her face looked like it had been stretched back till her eyes were where her ears used to be. She looked surprised. Permanently.

I guess it was the look she was going for.

"Thank you for taking such good care of my little Princess," Mrs. Vernaglia said. "You even brought me her wormy deposit."

"If you only knew what I had to go through to get it," I said softly.

I turned and walked away.

Princess came bounding after me. I reached

down and patted her head. To my surprise, she licked my hand in true affection.

"See you tomorrow, Princess," I said.

I had reached the door when Princess decided to bark.

"Ruff! Ruff! Ruff!"

As I closed the door behind me I heard Mrs. Vernaglia shriek. "Oh! Oh! That's not my baby's voice! What has happened to my Princess!"

Princess would never be quite the same. I guess Mrs. Vernaglia would just have to learn to live with that.

I went out to the street, out into bright sunshine and a warm breeze.

I had a hundred bucks in my pocket. But I was alone.

Alone.

Until Dawn crossed the street.

"How did it go?" she asked.

"Perfect." I grinned. "That was an excellent idea you had. You know, about just picking up any old deposit in the park and tossing in an earthworm."

Dawn smiled. "Yeah. Like the old woman

was going to know the difference."

"I got the money."

"And we're still friends," Dawn said. "There must be a moral here, somewhere."

"Sure," I said. I took Dawn's hand and held it. "The moral is that there really is something more important than money. Friendship. But hey, if you can have friends *and* money, well, why not?"

Dawn smiled. She has a great smile.

"Come on, Albert. We have an appointment to keep."

Together we walked along the boulevard to the doctor's office where, once we told him about our trip through the sewer, we were each given forty-seven separate shots.

We were passing by a sewer drain when I swear I heard a far-off voice cry, "Keep looking, Biff! I know they're down here somewhere!"

"Did you hear that?" I asked Dawn.

"Nope."

"Me neither."

Glossary of Terms

barficane: *noun.* See Appendix A.

blew magoo: *noun.* To heave, vomit, extrude, blow, or hurl. As in, "I was so sick, I did the blew magoo." The origins of this phrase are lost in the mists of time.

brown substance: *noun.* The basic ingredient that goes into the making of diaper gravy and buttwurst.

Chihuahua chocolate: *noun.* See *dogwurst.*

diaper gravy: *noun.* The characteristic product of babies and one of the most deadly substances known to man.

dogwurst: *noun.* From the canine form of *buttwurst.* Named for its resemblance to other members of the "wurst" family, such as brat and knock, the traditional dogwurst differs in that it is not accompanied by either sauerkraut or mustard.

five regrettable fluids: The five regrettables, as they are sometimes called, are pukus, mucus, waximus auriculas, numero uno, and numero dos. In less formal terms they are gumbo, nose butter, ear orange, squirt, and pooptonium. (A more complete explanation of the history of the five regrettables can be found in Barf-O-Rama #4.)

gack dance: *noun.* The characteristic gagging that precedes an episode of hurling.

gumbo: *noun.* Not sure, but believed to involve okra.

guttal explosion: *noun.* An extrusion of stomach contents in an explosive fashion.

heave: *verb.* See *guttal explosion.*

Lassie loaf: *noun.* Similar to Benji bars or, more generally, dogwurst, the Lassie loaf is known for its ability to communicate information related to trouble at the old mine.

magoo: *1. noun.* Vomit, stomach contents, lunch revisited, gumbo. *2. verb.* To huff, hurl, chuck, extrude, vomit, heave, or blow.

megawad: *noun.* First theorized by Copernicus, the megawad is the combination of all the five regrettable fluids.

pooptonium: *noun.* A more deadly form of plutonium, originally developed as a by-product of the Manhattan Project.

Pukatoa: *noun.* A volcano usually described as being east of Java, it is actually west of Java. Or the reverse.

stomach contents: *noun.* The official, scientific term for barf and puke. As used in the *Journal of the American Medical Association.*

universal hufferage: *noun.* When a group, party, assemblage, or nation vomits as one.

Appendix A
The Official Barficane Rating System*

Force 1: Gack dance occurs but subsides before any guttal explosion occurs.

Force 2: Gack dance is followed by a minor, internal hurl confined to the back of the mouth. Also known as a "pretaster."

Force 3: This is the basic "taster" in which stomach contents meet taste buds but do not reach the front teeth.

Force 4: The rawlf and recapture. A variation on the "taster." Spew reaches the mouth proper, is stopped by the lips and teeth, and is successfully reswallowed.

Force 5: This is the lowest level of actual puke launch. The barfoleum escapes through the teeth but is slowed sufficiently so that no airborne launch occurs. The gumbo dribbles down the chin.

Force 6: The basic barf. This is a no-frills vomitation. Hurling occurs with minimal force. Floor mats are extra.

Force 7: Puke storm. Levels 7 through 10 are true puke storms. At level 7 the gumbo goes airborne. It may strike other objects or individuals. Dentures or loose teeth may be blown out.

Force 8: The so-called fire hose. A powerful, focused stream of chunks is launched at maximum speed. In rare cases it may knock the vomiteer off his feet and even propel him around the room. It can also strip paint off old furniture.

Force 9: Pukatoa. There are huge amounts of relatively low-impact hurl, buckets and buckets of gumbo defying all laws of physics. In some cases the volume of barf has been greater than the actual weight of the heaver. (Low-lying coastal areas should be evacuated.)

Force 10: The infamous rocket rawlf. This is a very rare and very dangerous phenomenon that combines the sheer volume of a Pukatoa with the power of the fire hose. Minor internal organs (the pancreas, liver, and intestines) may be extruded. Innocent bystanders may be severely injured by the force of the explosive gumbo stream. There is extreme danger of flooding. Mobile homes are especially vulnerable.

*Reprinted from National Weather Service Bulletin #312-BF-6654790/1996

HERE'S A SNEAK PEEK AT **BARF-O-RAMA** #6, TO WEE OR NOT TO WEE.

But soft! What whiff through yonder hinder breaks?

— Shakespew, Barf of Avon

"Hey, Alotsa Snotsa, what part are you trying out for? *Juliet?*" Bryan asked me.

"That's real funny, Bryan," I said. I grinned at the joke. Two jokes, actually. The one where he made fun of my name, which is really Alonzo. And the joke where he acted like maybe I would try out for a girl's part in the school play.

"Hah hah hah," I laughed.

Bryan is a very funny guy. He's also my best friend. But if you're going to hang around with someone as cool as Bryan, you have to get used to having him make jokes about you.

I mean, I guess my name *is* kind of funny. Alonzo. I'm the only Alonzo in school.

We were standing in the mostly empty school auditorium. There were maybe a dozen or two dozen kids there, more girls than boys. Plus Mr. Stipe, the teacher. He was the teacher in charge of the school play. The play was *Romeo and Juliet*.

It's by Shakespeare. I guess it's sort of famous. Even though it's a "love" play. You know, a romance.

"I'm going to be Romeo," Bryan said.

This surprised me. Bryan in a play? "I didn't think you were even interested in drama," I said.

"Drama?" He made a face. "Oh, you mean this play. You moron, of course I'm not interested in the play. It's just that it will get me out of English class and Ms. Holland hates me. She'll give me an F in English. But if I do this play, *this* will be my English grade. Ha hah! Pretty smart, huh?"

"Yeah. Really smart."

"Really smart. Reeeelly sma-art," Bryan

said, making fun of the way I said it.

Which I guess was funny. Bryan thought so, anyway. So I laughed along.

It's a good idea to laugh at Bryan's jokes. Bryan gets upset if you don't laugh at his jokes. And when he gets upset there's trouble.

Bryan is kind of big, in case you didn't guess that already. And he's tough. And mean. Kind of mean. But in a funny way.

"So. What are *you* doing here, Snotsa?" Bryan asked.

I shrugged. "Same as you. I was going to be in the play so I could get out of regular English."

"You zithead. That's so stupid. You already have, like, an A in English. Besides, who's ever going to give *you* a part?"

"I guess you're right," I said meekly. "I probably won't get it."

"I know why you want it," Bryan said. "It's because Kelly Armstrong is playing the part of Juliet and whoever is Romeo gets to kiss her."

"No way!" I yelled so loudly that half the other kids turned to stare.

Okay, look, maybe I did kind of like Kelly. But that wasn't the only reason I wanted to be in the play. Most of the reason, but not the only reason.

Then Bryan made a face, like something was the matter. He started patting his hinder. Nothing unusual for Bryan.

"Hey!" he said, "I think I have a hole in my jeans."

"A hole in your jeans?"

"Yeah. Take a look for me, will you?" He bent over and aimed his big reek cheeks at me.

I leaned over to look for the hole. I guess I should have known what to expect.

BLAAAT!

I was so close I felt the deadly wind of his buttnado!

"Aaaarrrgghh!" I cried.

"Hah hah hah hah! Oh, that was beautiful!" Bryan crowed. "I totally nailed you. Hah hah hah hah!"

I was still reeling from the morbific stench. Bryan is a guy who likes to eat things like sausage and cheese and potato salad. When he farts, the whole world knows about it.

"I can't *believe* you fell for that," Bryan said. "How come you're such an idiot?"

"I—I—d-don't know," I managed to gasp as I tried to suck in some unpolluted oxygen.

"It's a good thing you have me to look out for you," Bryan said. Then he grabbed me around the neck.

I tried to squirm free, but he had me good.

"Noogie! Noogie! Noogie!" Bryan yelled as he knuckled my head.

It hurt, but only a baby would yell or cry or whatever.

"Hey, you two! What's going on over there?" It was Mr. Stipe.

"Nothing," Bryan said.

"Well, it doesn't look like nothing," Mr. Stipe said. "Are you okay, Alonzo?"

Bryan let me up so I could say, "We're just messing around, Mr. Stipe."

"Well, we're not here to mess around," Mr. Stipe said. "We're here for tryouts for the play. What part are you going to read for, Alonzo?"

I cringed. "Um . . . Romeo, I guess."

I looked at Bryan. He just shook his head like I was pathetic.

Which I was, I guess. I mean, that's what Bryan always says. And he's the coolest guy in school, so he would know.

"Good luck, Alonzo," Bryan said very sincerely. He even patted me on the back.

Which was nice, since he wanted to be Romeo too.

I practically crawled up on the stage. I was still gagging from Bryan's deadly fartillery. My hair was sticking up in the air from the noogie. But I felt better because he had said "good luck."

I crept onto the stage. Kelly Armstrong was already standing there bathed in a soft glow of spotlights. Her blond hair seemed to form a halo around her head. She looked like an angel.

I stumbled crossing the stage. But Kelly smiled at me, and kind of shook her head. In a sympathetic way, you know? Like she was saying, It's okay, everyone stumbles sometimes.

I stood just a few feet away from her. I'd never been that close to her before. She was beautiful up close.

I swallowed hard. I tried to remember my lines. I'd stayed up late memorizing them. And I said:

"Oh, she doth teach the torches to burn bright.
It seems she hangs upon the cheek of night
Like a rich jewel in Ethiop's ear;
Beauty too rich for use, for earth too dear!"

I had more lines, but then I realized people were laughing. People out in the audience, the other kids.

But some were not laughing. Instead they were going, "Eewwww, gross!"

I stopped, confused. Had I done something dumb?

Then I felt it. Something brushing my back.

I reached over my shoulder, and my fingers touched a sheet of paper. Someone had taped a piece of paper to my back.

I pulled it off and looked at it.

It was a Xerox copy of my face, all squished

up. There was a big river of snot flowing from my nose.

I remembered the day. I'd had a bad cold. Bryan had grabbed my head and forced my face down on the Xerox machine. Then he had taken a copy of my smushed, snotty face.

Now that picture was on my back.

"Alotsa Snotsa!" Bryan crowed gleefully from the audience. "I hope Kelly doesn't mind kissing *that* face! Ha hah!"

We hope you enjoyed reading this book. If you would like to receive further information about available titles in the Bantam series, just write to the address below, with your name and address:

KIM PRIOR
Bantam Books
61–63 Uxbridge Road
London W5 5SA

If you live in Australia or New Zealand and would like more information about the series, please write to:

SALLY PORTER
Transworld Publishers (Australia) Pty Ltd
15–25 Helles Avenue
Moorebank
NSW 2170
AUSTRALIA

KIRI MARTIN
Transworld Publishers (NZ) Ltd
3 William Pickering Drive
Albany
Auckland
NEW ZEALAND

All Transworld titles are available by post from:
Bookservice by Post, PO Box 29,
Douglas, Isle of Man IM99 1BQ

Credit Cards accepted.
Please telephone 01624 675137, fax 01624 670923
or Internet http://www.bookpost.co.uk
or e-mail: bookshop@enterprise.net for details

Free postage and packing in the UK.
Overseas customers: allow £1 per book (paperbacks)
and £3 per book (hardbacks).